The Umbrella Tree

Copyright © 2021 by Shanghai Press and Publishing Development Co., Ltd.
Chinese edition:
Text Copyright © Bai Bing
Illustration Copyright © Li Hongzhuan
First published in 2016 in China by China Children's Press & Publication Group

All rights reserved. Unauthorized reproduction, in any manner, is prohibited.

This book is edited and designed by the Editorial Committee of *Cultural China* series.

Story by Bai Bing
Illustrations by Li Hongzhuan
Translation by Yijin Wert

Copy Editor: Shelly Bryant
Editor: Cao Yue
Editorial Director: Zhang Yicong

Senior Consultants: Sun Yong, Wu Ying, Yang Xinci
Managing Director and Publisher: Wang Youbu

ISBN: 978-1-60220-464-5

Address any comments about *The Umbrella Tree* to:

Better Link Press
99 Park Ave
New York, NY 10016
USA

or

Shanghai Press and Publishing Development Co., Ltd.
F 7 Donghu Road, Shanghai, China (200031)
Email: comments_betterlinkpress@hotmail.com

Printed in China by Shanghai Donnelley Printing Co., Ltd.

1   3   5   7   9   10   8   6   4   2

The Umbrella Tree

A Story Told in English and Chinese

雨伞树

By Bai Bing & Li Hongzhuan

Translated by Yijin Wert

Better Link Press

Guagua and his younger sister Yaya had a very old red umbrella. They hung a little stuffed panda on their beloved umbrella. The red umbrella liked to shelter the two pandas from the wind and rain.

熊猫哥哥瓜瓜和妹妹丫丫有一把很旧、很旧的红雨伞,他们在心爱的伞上挂了一个小小的布熊猫。红雨伞也喜欢给兄妹俩遮风挡雨。

One day, a gust of heavy wind blew the red umbrella onto the top of a tree, tearing the umbrella to pieces and destroying the frame. Guagua and Yaya were very upset.

一天，红雨伞被一阵大风刮到了树上，划出好多口子，伞骨也散了。瓜瓜和丫丫好伤心。

"Will you be able to repair the red umbrella?" Yaya asked her mother after she got home.
"Let me try!" her mother replied.

回到家,丫丫问妈妈:"我们的红雨伞能修好吗?"
妈妈说:"试试吧。"

A few days later, it rained again. They saw a new floral umbrella in the umbrella holder, but they could not find their own red umbrella.

过几天,又下雨了。可是红雨伞不见了,伞架上是把新的花雨伞。

"I want our red umbrella!" Yaya said.

"I want our red umbrella, too!" Guagua said.

"I couldn't repair your red umbrella, so I threw her into the trash can. If you want her, you may be able to find her there," their mother answered.

丫丫说:"我要红雨伞!"

瓜瓜说:"我也要我们的红雨伞!"

妈妈说:"红雨伞修不好了,我把她扔进了垃圾箱,你们去找,或许还找得到!"

But their red umbrella had been loaded onto a garbage truck by Uncle Black Bear who transported her to a remote garbage dump.

When they couldn't find their red umbrella, Guagua and Yaya were so sad that they started to cry.

可是,红雨伞被黑熊伯伯装上垃圾车,运去了很远的垃圾场。

瓜瓜和丫丫没找到红雨伞,难过地哭了。

The little monkey got the red umbrella. He danced with her. The little deer got the red umbrella. She rode on her. The little fox got the red umbrella. He ran with her and then threw her on the ground.

小猴子捡到了红雨伞，挥呀舞呀。梅花鹿捡到了红雨伞，骑呀骑呀。小狐狸捡到了红雨伞，跑呀跑呀，然后把她扔到了地上。

The red umbrella was very sad. She cried herself to sleep. In her dream, she found herself becoming a new umbrella covering the heads of Guagua and Yaya.

红雨伞很伤心,流着泪睡着了。梦中她变成了新伞,罩在瓜瓜和丫丫的头上。

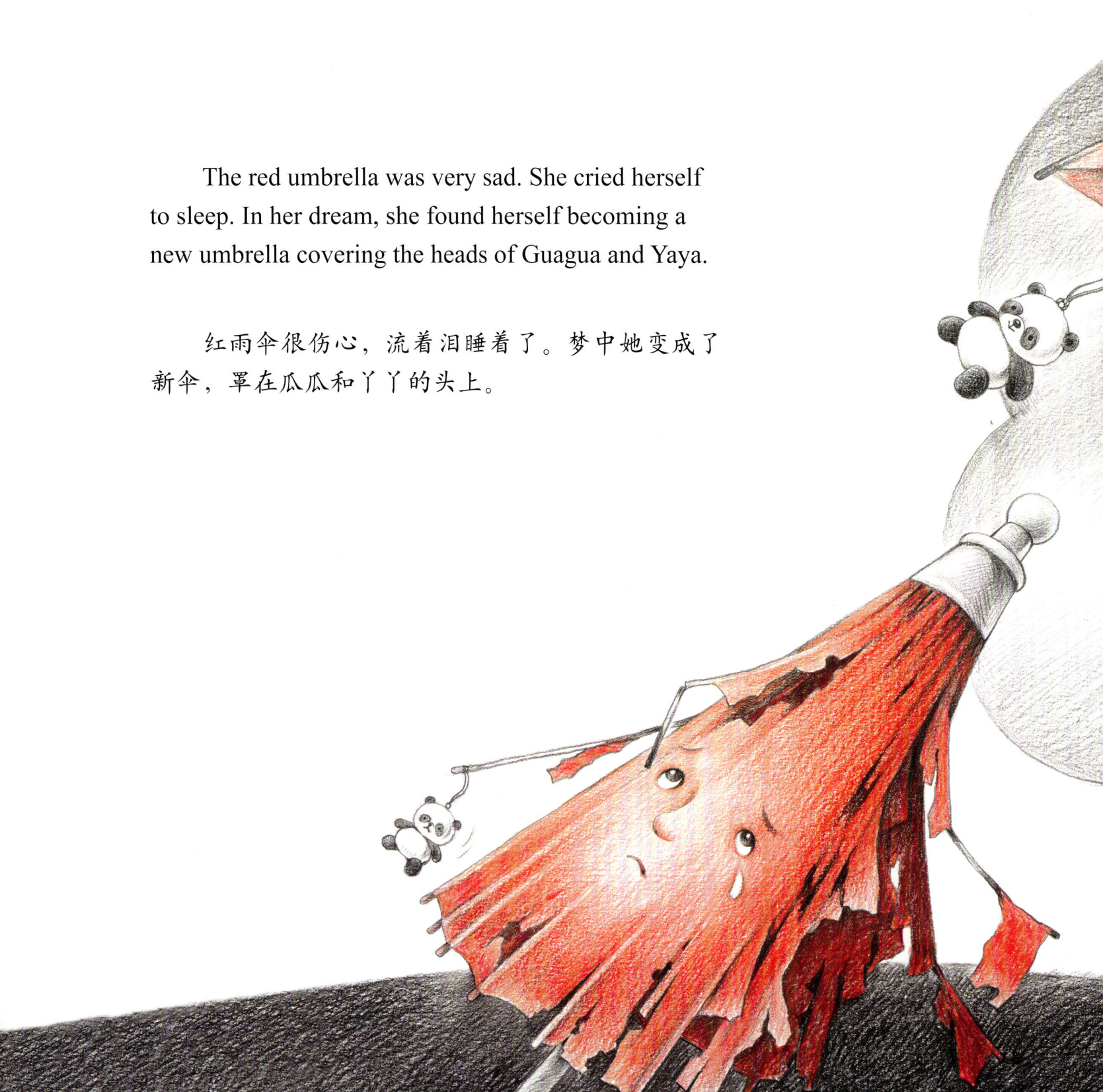

When she woke up, the red umbrella found new roots sprouting out of her. She grew and grew and soon became a big, strong umbrella tree.

醒来后，红雨伞发现自己长出了根须，发出了嫩芽。她长啊长啊，很快长成一棵又高又粗的雨伞树。

Soon her branches were full of flowers.
Every flower was a small red umbrella.

不久,她的枝杈上开满了花朵。每一朵花都是一把小红伞。

A little wild donkey came. He picked up a small red umbrella.

A group of swans and big birds also came. They picked up the small red umbrellas.

小野驴来了，捡起了一把小红伞。

天鹅和大鸟也飞来了，衔起了一把把小红伞……

One day, Guagua and Yaya saw the little wild donkey holding a small red umbrella. "She looks very familiar. Where did you get her?" they asked.

"There is a big umbrella tree on that mountain," the little donkey replied.

一天,瓜瓜和丫丫看见了小野驴手里的小红伞:"这伞好面熟呀,在哪儿买的?"

小野驴说:"山上有棵雨伞树。"

Guagua and Yaya ran to the tree. Guagua picked up a small red umbrella. "What a beautiful small red umbrella! But I still want my old red umbrella back!" Yaya said.

瓜瓜和丫丫跑过去。瓜瓜捡起一把小红伞，丫丫说："多好看的小红伞！可是，我还是想找到原来的那把红雨伞！"

Suddenly, Yaya shouted, " Look, Brother!" Their little stuffed panda was hanging on one of the branches.

突然,丫丫喊:"哥哥,你快看!"树枝上,挂着他们的小小布熊猫。

Hugging the umbrella tree tightly, Yaya and Guagua asked, "Red Umbrella, is that really you? We finally found you!"

The red umbrella thought she was dreaming, but she felt the warmth on the face of the pandas. This was real!

丫丫和瓜瓜紧紧搂着雨伞树说:"是你吗,红雨伞?可找到你了!"

红雨伞以为自己在做梦,可是,她感觉到了熊猫脸蛋的温暖。这是真的!

Lying against the tree under its shade, Guagua and Yaya fell asleep, surrounded by many small red umbrellas.

瓜瓜和丫丫坐在树荫下,靠着雨伞树睡着了,身边落满了红红的小雨伞。

Cultural Explanation
知识点

Giant Panda　大熊猫

The giant panda is categorized under the first class of animal protection law in China. It has distinctive black-and-white fur with a round body. Its temperament is docile. It loves to eat bamboo and enjoys playing.

中国特有的一级保护动物，毛色黑白相间，身体圆滚滚，性情温顺，爱吃竹子，喜爱嬉戏。

Oil-Paper Umbrella　油纸伞

The oil-paper umbrella not only can be used to provide protection from rain, it is also a form of traditional Chinese artwork. The umbrella frame is usually made from bamboo. The top of the umbrella can be covered with paintings or poems before the paper is sealed with tung oil. Originating in China, the oil-paper umbrella was later introduced to neighboring countries such as Japan.

不仅是日常雨具，也是中国的传统工艺品，用竹条做伞骨，以涂上桐油的纸做伞面，伞面上可题诗作画。发明于中国，后逐渐传至日本等邻国。

Key Word
关键词

Companionship　陪伴

Everyone has their own "red umbrella." It could be an item or a person. With its companionship, we do not feel lonely. Instead, our hearts are filled with love and warmth.

每个人都有属于自己的"小红伞"，或是一件物品，或是一个人。有它的陪伴，我们不觉得孤单，心中充满爱与温暖。